THE CASE OF THE QUESTIONABLE COUSIN

Elizabeth Bryan Mysteries

Vicki Berger Erwin

SAINT LOUIS

To a special group of friends
who keep me in stitches:
Ellen, Gail, Janet,
Kathy, and Mary Ann.

Special thank
to Ellen Harms
for her lessons on blood types
and to Ruth Geisler
for her unflagging support
and encouragement
on this project.

Elizabeth Bryan Mysteries
The Disappearing Card Trick
The Case of the Questionable Cousin

Cover illustration by Sally Schaedler

Copyright © 1996 Concordia Publishing House
3558 S. Jefferson Avenue, St. Louis, MO 63118-3968
Manufactured in the United States of America

Library of Congress Cataloging-in-Publication Data

Erwin, Vicki Berger, 1951–

    The case of the questionable cousin / Vicki Berger Erwin.
      p.   cm. — (Elizabeth Bryan mysteries)
    Summary: Elizabeth's work on blood types for her science fair pro-
ject proves valuable when she becomes suspicious of the young woman
who has appeared claiming to be Aunt Nan's niece.
    ISBN 0-570-04836-2
    [1. Mystery and detective stories. 2. Christian life—Fiction. 3. Science
projects—Fiction.] I. Title. II. Series.
PZ7.E7445Cas 1996
[Fic]—dc 20
                                      95-22849

2 3 4 5 6 7 8 9 10   05 04 03 02 01 00 99 98 97 96

CONTENTS

1
A STRANGER KNOCKS

"Blood!" Elizabeth stared down at the book she had been paging through.

"Gross," Meghan said. She continued to paint her fingernails bright pink without a glance at what Elizabeth pored over.

"No, I think this one will work. I'm going to do my science fair project on blood types. Look." Elizabeth shoved the book under Meghan's nose.

"This is your science fair project—not mine. Get those disgusting pictures away from me." Meghan held her hands, fingernails shining with fresh polish, up in the air and twisted her body away from Elizabeth and the open book.

"You have to do a project too, you know," Elizabeth said. She pulled her feet up onto the bed and leaned against the wall.

"The science fair is too far away to worry about." Meghan blew on her wet nails.

"It's next week!"

"So, I'll work on my project this weekend."

"Amy Catherine has been working on her project for months," said Elizabeth. "She wins every year. I wish this one time ..."

"Amy Catherine's *mother* has been working on her project for months," Meghan reminded her.

"My project is going to be better than hers this year," Elizabeth said.

"Let me braid your hair." Meghan picked up Elizabeth's hairbrush.

Elizabeth pulled her head away. "My hair's dirty," she mumbled.

"That's when it's easiest to braid."

Without looking up from the book, Elizabeth scooted closer so Meghan could reach her hair.

"I love your red hair. Mine is so boring. Brown. Ugh!" said Meghan.

"Your hair is perfectly fine," said Elizabeth.

"I wish my mom would let me color it."

"Don't you dare!"

"I know. I'll do my science project on hair

dyes. How much hair dye does it really take to ruin your hair? Or if you use red hair color on black hair, what happens? Or what happens if you use red dye, then blond dye, then brown? It'll work, won't it? Maybe I can convince my mom that my hair won't fall out if I color it one time."

"Where will you get the hair? And the dye?" Elizabeth asked.

"You could give me some of your hair. I could ask other people for theirs. I could buy the dye or maybe use the leftovers from a beauty shop," Meghan said.

"You are *not* getting any of my hair." Elizabeth pulled away, but Meghan followed, not letting go of the half-finished braid.

"You're the only person I know with red hair. You have to help me," Meghan begged.

"And you'll give me some blood in exchange?"

"Blood? You want my blood? How are you going to get it? What are you going to do with it?" Meghan let go of the braid.

"I really only need to know your blood type," said Elizabeth.

"Maybe my mom knows. I don't think I want any needles stuck in me." Meghan finished the braid.

"I'm going to do blood types and families. What blood type will a child have based on the blood types of its parents. It could be kind of like a game," Elizabeth explained.

"Do you know your blood type?" Meghan asked.

"Mom will know," said Elizabeth.

"Do you know Justin's blood type? You could figure out what blood type your children will have," Meghan said, then giggled.

Elizabeth felt her face get hot. "I don't think so. Justin is a friend. Like you." She and Justin had become friends last summer when they tangled with a dishonest baseball card dealer. Everyone teased her about her boyfriend, but she insisted that he was a boy *friend*.

"Yeah, right. Well, you could try to figure out what blood type kids your mom and Mr. Hamilton would have. Would they be the same as you and Mike?"

"I don't think so again," said Elizabeth. Her mother had started dating for the first time since her father died five years ago. Elizabeth wasn't sure she liked the man her mom had chosen— Don Hamilton, a high school teacher and her younger brother's baseball coach. She guessed he was perfectly nice, but she didn't know if she was ready for someone who seemed to be taking her father's place with everybody except her.

"Look in the mirror. Your hair is darling." Meghan guided Elizabeth to the bathroom.

Meghan never did stick with one subject long. It was one of the things Elizabeth both liked and disliked about her best friend. It kept Elizabeth on her toes, and at the same time, it drove her crazy.

Her hair did look good. Elizabeth fluffed her bangs.

Meghan stood on her tiptoes and moved into the mirror next to Elizabeth. She held her dark braid against Elizabeth's lighter braid. "How could we get them the same color?"

An orange cat jumped up on the sink, and Elizabeth turned on the faucet. The cat stuck his head down and lapped at the fresh running water.

"Your cats are so spoiled!" said Meghan.

Elizabeth smiled, then waited until the cat finished drinking and jumped down before she turned off the water.

"Aren't you glad you came over to study?"

Elizabeth asked. "Now you have your science project all figured out."

Meghan stuffed her books into her backpack. "How did you do that? I hadn't even thought about the science fair before today, except about how far away it was, and I guess it's not that far away."

"It's a gift," Elizabeth said, then giggled. "I did the same thing to Justin. He's going to do something about throwing a baseball."

"Surprise, surprise. Walk me to the corner?"

"I'll cut a little hair out from underneath if you really need it for your project," Elizabeth said.

"Let me figure out what I'm going to do first. But thanks. How many friends would give the hair off their heads?"

"How many would give their *blood?*"

"I never said … Hey, who's that woman on your porch?"

Elizabeth looked out the window at a short woman with waist-length, straight, dark hair, wearing a denim jacket, jeans, and western boots. She was standing in front of the door to the neighboring half of the duplex, where Elizabeth's Aunt Nan lived. Aunt Nan wasn't really her aunt. She was more of an adopted grand-mother to Elizabeth and her brother, Mike.

The woman knocked on Aunt Nan's door, then turned and stared out toward the street.

"Is Mrs. Albright home?" Meghan asked.

Elizabeth shook her head. "Aunt Nan and Mom took Mike to the library."

Just then, the woman moved across to the door to Elizabeth's house. She lifted her hand, and Elizabeth found herself eye to eye with the stranger.

Opening the door a crack, Elizabeth asked, "May I help you?"

"Is Nan Albright around? Do you know where she is?" The woman, who looked younger close up, sounded irritated that Aunt Nan wasn't home.

"She should be back any minute. I'll give her a message, if you want," Elizabeth offered.

The woman let out a long, loud sigh. Without a word to Elizabeth, she moved to the porch swing and sat down.

Elizabeth closed the door, making sure to turn the lock. "You can't go home yet," she said to Meghan.

"My mom will be calling the police." The

two girls looked at one another.

Elizabeth glanced over her shoulder. Through the window she could see the woman sitting motionless on the swing. She *seemed* perfectly harmless.

"We'll wait a few minutes to see if Aunt Nan and Mom come home. They should be here any time." At that moment, a car turned into the drive.

Elizabeth felt weak with relief. She twisted the lock and opened the door.

The woman was already down the steps and on her way to the car by the time Elizabeth and Meghan got outside.

"Aunt Nan?" the woman asked.

The older woman paused, half in and half out of the car.

"It's Dede, Aunt Nan. Helen's daughter."

Aunt Nan's eyes widened, then her mouth dropped open, closed, and opened again.

Dede threw her arms around the small, white-haired woman and held on.

Aunt Nan slowly raised her arms and patted the young woman's back. She pulled away and looked Dede up and down, once, twice, three times.

"Dede?" Aunt Nan's voice sounded hoarse.

"Helen's Dede?"

Stepping backward, Dede held her arms out, then turned around slowly.

"Mrs. Albright is her *real* aunt?" whispered Meghan.

Mom had joined Aunt Nan and Dede, shaking Dede's hand and moving them toward the house.

"Hi, Meghan, Elizabeth, this is Dede Carter, Aunt Nan's niece from Santa Fe, New Mexico," Mom said.

"Pleased to meet you," Meghan said.

"Hi," said Elizabeth. Her younger brother, Mike, stood close by Elizabeth's side, staring at Dede like she was an exhibit at the zoo.

"Come on in," Mom invited everyone. "Nan looks like she could use some tea, and I know I could."

Aunt Nan's normally pink cheeks were papery white, and her lips were trembling. Elizabeth took her hand, surprised by its chilliness, and walked with Aunt Nan to the kitchen. Once there, Aunt Nan slowly sank into the first chair she reached. Elizabeth stood behind her, her hands on Aunt Nan's shoulders.

"I didn't see your car," Mom said to Dede as

she turned on the burner under the teakettle.

"I came on the bus and walked from the station. Well, it's not exactly a station, it's a Hardee's. I asked at a gas station for directions," said Dede. She talked to Mom but glanced at Aunt Nan from time to time.

"I don't know what to say," Aunt Nan finally spoke. "Helen's baby. I haven't seen you since you ..."

Dede reached over and patted Aunt Nan's hand. "I know," she said. They looked at each other, and Elizabeth knew somehow they were saying something no one else in the room could hear.

Mom set four cups on the table. "Meghan, do you drink tea?"

Elizabeth's head whipped around. She'd forgotten about Meghan.

"I'd better get home," Meghan said, but she made no move toward the door.

Mom looked at the clock.

"See you at school tomorrow," Elizabeth said.

Meghan backed away. "Call me," she mouthed.

Elizabeth nodded.

Mike moved to the edge of the table between Aunt Nan and Dede. He looked from one to the other without saying a word. Elizabeth wondered what had gotten into him. Usually he talked constantly.

Aunt Nan pushed her chair back. "Lydia, I appreciate your help getting us through these first difficult moments, but I think Dede and I have a few things to discuss between ourselves."

Dede stood up too.

As the two of them walked out of the room, Aunt Nan put her arm around Dede's waist and pulled her close. "Helen's little girl," Elizabeth heard her say again.

The front door closed, then Aunt Nan's door opened and shut.

"Does this mean Aunt Nan isn't *our* aunt anymore?" Mike asked.

The teakettle whistled shrilly.

HEARD
IN THE HALL

Mom leaned down and hugged Mike tightly. "No, no, no," she said.

Elizabeth, unable to bear the shrill whistle, pulled the kettle off the stove and poured the steaming water into Mom's mug.

"Aunt Nan will *always* be our Aunt Nan," Mom said to Mike. "An aunt can have any number of nieces and nephews and love them all. Just like a mother has more love as she has more children. She doesn't have a given amount that she has to divide among her kids. The love multiplies. Just like God doesn't divide His love. He loves us all the same."

"But *she's* Aunt Nan's real niece," Elizabeth said.

"I don't think Nan thinks like that at all," Mom assured Elizabeth.

"Is Dede our cousin then?" Mike asked.

"No!" Elizabeth and Mom answered at the same time.

"Why didn't Aunt Nan know who she was?" asked Elizabeth.

Mom let go of Mike and sat down at the table. She pulled her cup of tea in front of her and added a spoonful of sugar, then stirred.

"Dede's mother, Helen, was Aunt Nan's younger sister. They lived in New Mexico, maybe Arizona. Helen died of leukemia when Dede was 5 or 6 years old, and her father took Dede and disappeared. Aunt Nan tried to find them, but she never could. She probably thought she'd never see Dede again."

Someone knocked on the front door. Mike ran to answer.

"Let me get it, sweetie," Mom said.

Elizabeth stared at the science book she'd carried downstairs as Meghan was leaving. Perhaps she could use Aunt Nan and Dede in her science experiment, Elizabeth thought.

Mom returned to the kitchen followed by her friend, Don Hamilton.

"Guess what?" Mike said to the tall, dark-haired man. "Aunt Nan has a brand-new niece."

Mr. Hamilton patted Mike on the shoulder. "That's what your mother said. Pretty exciting, huh?"

Yeah, right, thought Elizabeth.

Mike shrugged. By his silence, Elizabeth could tell her little brother wasn't quite sure what was happening.

"Hey, Mikey, let's go play ..." Elizabeth started to say.

"*Don't* call me Mikey. I'm Mike," her brother said between clenched teeth.

"Hi, Elizabeth," Mr. Hamilton said.

"Hi, Mr. Hamilton," Elizabeth answered politely. She even managed to smile. She wondered why he was stopping by right at dinnertime—again. He managed to find some excuse to see her mother nearly every day. And Mom didn't do anything to discourage him. She wouldn't allow Elizabeth to do anything either.

Picking up her book, Elizabeth started to leave.

"Did you decide on a science fair project?" Mom asked, pointing at the book.

"I'm thinking of doing blood types," said Elizabeth. She'd hoped to be able to discuss the whole project with Mom, but now that Mr.

Hamilton had arrived, Mom wouldn't have any time for her.

"I might be able to help you," said Mr. Hamilton. "When I was in college, I worked in a hospital laboratory. One of the things I learned was how to type blood."

"I'm not going to do the blood tests," said Elizabeth. "But thanks for the offer," she added quickly. Mom *insisted* she be polite to the intruder, as Elizabeth thought of Mr. Hamilton.

"What *are* you going to do?" Mom asked.

"I'm going to make up a game. The rules will be the 'rules' about blood types. Like, the O factor is recessive. Then the object will be to figure out what's missing in the family grouping. Maybe I'll have the dad's type and the kid's type, and you'll have to figure out the mom's type." Once she started talking about the project, Elizabeth couldn't stop.

"Each type will have a different color and players can stick pins in the square …"

"It's called a Punnett square," Mr. Hamilton interrupted.

"Whatever," said Elizabeth. She decided she'd tell Mom the rest later. "I have homework. How long until supper?"

"I'd invited Don to join us for spaghetti, but then Dede showed up," said Mom.

"I'll go get some burgers," said Mr. Hamilton. "We can get enough for Nan and this girl too."

"Burger King," said Mike, grabbing Mr. Hamilton's hand and jumping up and down. "Please?"

"Won't argue with that," said Mr. Hamilton. "It's my favorite."

"Mine too," said Mike.

To Elizabeth's disappointment, Mike liked Mr. Hamilton as much as Mom did. She'd prayed and prayed for God's help to deal with the problem of Mr. Hamilton, and the way things were going, God would continue to hear from her about the man.

"Earth to Elizabeth? Are you there?" Mom snapped her fingers in front of Elizabeth's face.

"What?" Elizabeth stepped back.

"Burger King okay with you?" Mom asked.

"Fine. Whopper Jr., fries, and a Coke," said Elizabeth. She could get some homework done while Mr. Hamilton went to pick up the meal.

"Whopper Jr., fries, and *milk*," Mom said. She picked up the phone and dialed Aunt Nan's number.

Elizabeth started to leave again.

"It's busy. Elizabeth, run next door to see if Aunt Nan wants Don to pick up some dinner for her too," asked Mom, hanging up the phone.

"Mom, do I have to?" Elizabeth asked. She knew she sounded whiny.

"Yes, it's only over to Aunt Nan's, as close as your own room."

Elizabeth knew from the tone of Mom's voice it wouldn't do any good to argue. She wasn't sure why she was so reluctant to go to Aunt Nan's anyway. She and Mike spent almost as much time next door as they spent in their own house. The houses were mirror images, and she usually felt as at home in one as the other.

"Tonight, Elizabeth," Mom said.

The front door to Aunt Nan's was open. Elizabeth put her hand on the screen-door handle, then hesitated. She and Mike walked in and out of Aunt Nan's without knocking all the time. Yet she knocked softly this time. No one appeared, and the house seemed unusually quiet.

Elizabeth opened the screen door and stepped inside. She walked across the living room toward the kitchen. She saw Dede's back, the telephone cradled against her shoulder.

"Not a clue, I tell you. She's perfect, asking all the right questions—the ones I can answer," Dede said, then laughed softly.

"Lizzybeth? Was that you knocking on the door? Since when do you bother to knock? Where's Dede? Did she let you inside?" asked Aunt Nan from the hallway leading to the bedrooms. "I was in the bathroom. My stomach is feeling full of rocks this evening." She hugged Elizabeth tightly.

Dede turned as soon as she heard Aunt Nan's voice and looked at Elizabeth, her eyes narrowing. She spoke into the phone again, then hung up quickly.

"Who were you talking to, my dear?" Aunt Nan asked.

"I was calling to check on my kittens. I hated leaving them, but they're fine," Dede answered.

Elizabeth tried to make the bit of conversation she'd heard fit into Dede's explanation. What did asking the right questions have to do with kittens? She looked at Dede again only to find the young woman staring at her. Dede's icy blue eyes chilled Elizabeth.

"Mom wants to know if you'd like Mr. Hamilton to pick up some Burger King for you when he goes to get ours," Elizabeth asked Aunt Nan.

Aunt Nan walked slowly to the sofa and sat down. "Nothing for me. I don't feel well." She laid her hand on her stomach.

"What's wrong?" She'd been so anxious to keep an eye on Dede, Elizabeth realized she'd barely looked at Aunt Nan. Now that she was paying attention, the older woman looked pale and deep lines were etched across her forehead and around her eyes. "You want me to get Mom?" Elizabeth asked.

Aunt Nan chuckled. "It's a little tummy-ache. Comes and goes. I'll be fine in the morning. Dede, how about you? Could Elizabeth get you a sandwich?"

"No, thank you. I *never* eat meat. And Aunt Nan, I have just the thing for your stomach. I'll brew you a special herbal tea that will set you right in no time," said Dede, already in the kitchen.

Elizabeth heard Dede opening and shutting cupboard doors and drawers.

"Elizabeth, you go on now and don't worry

about a thing. I'll take care of my Aunt Nan," Dede called out from the kitchen.

Aunt Nan kissed Elizabeth on the forehead. "Go on now. I'm sure you have homework. You heard Dede. She'll take care of me."

Elizabeth walked slowly back to her house, worried that was exactly what Dede might do.

3
WEIRD
SUSPICIONS

Elizabeth leaned against her locker in the school hallway and drew a big square in her notebook. Then she divided it into four smaller squares. "It's a Punnett square, and it's a big part of my science project. You use it to figure out the odds of a certain blood type happening. That's my science project." Elizabeth explained the drawing as Justin looked at it.

"Four squares? Will they have blood samples in them? Where are you going to get the blood?" Justin asked.

"Not real blood, but they will have something in them. I haven't decided what yet," said Elizabeth. "I do know it's going to be a good project." She stuck her empty lunch bag in her locker and slammed the door hard.

Meghan ran up to them, her brown hair

bouncing. "I thought I was going to miss you. I got stuck behind Amy Catherine when I went to get my science project approved. I had to listen to her give Mrs. Harms a progress report, mainly what supplies she'd bought for her project already," she said. "I was afraid I was going to miss my lunch period, so I ate my sandwich while I was waiting."

"Is your project about food?" Justin asked. "It would be a natural."

"No, it's about hair dyes, and I need a few of your golden locks to make it work." Meghan pulled on the stubbly blond hair sticking out from underneath Justin's baseball cap. "Or we could use your whole head."

"You want my hair. She wants my blood. These science fair projects could take a lot out of me," Justin said.

Elizabeth gave him a push. "You're going to be late for class."

"I'll call you tonight," Justin said. "I can't wait to hear more about the adventures of type A and type O!"

Elizabeth pushed him again.

"And I waited all night for you to call and tell me what happened after I left last night.

Who was that woman?" Meghan asked.

Elizabeth groaned. "You've waited this long. You can wait till after school."

"What woman?" Justin asked. "And it can't wait till after school. I have basketball practice."

"Some woman showed up at Elizabeth's Aunt Nan's house and said Aunt Nan was *her* aunt," said Meghan.

"So?" said Justin.

"Aunt Nan didn't recognize her," Elizabeth explained. "She hadn't seen her since she was really young, and Aunt Nan has never mentioned having any nieces or nephews to me."

"So she really *is* her niece?" Meghan asked.

"Looks that way. But there's something weird." Elizabeth saw her two friends exchange looks.

"What?" Meghan demanded.

"You think everything is weird since you caught Mr. Becker selling those counterfeit baseball cards," said Justin.

"I do not!"

"What about those 'weird' packages Mrs. Clark was sneaking around with at night?" asked Meghan.

"Her garbage," Justin reminded Elizabeth

with a laugh.

Elizabeth's face got warm. "But I heard Dede say to someone on the phone that Aunt Nan was asking all the right questions and that she, Aunt Nan, didn't have a clue. Then she told Aunt Nan she was talking to someone about her cats. And the look she gave me when she realized I'd overheard …" Relating the experience, Elizabeth felt the chilly blast of Dede's cold gaze all over again.

"She has cats; she can't be all bad," said Meghan.

"She was probably talking to a neighbor back home about something else—not cats and not her aunt," said Justin.

Elizabeth pressed her lips together to keep from saying anything else. She'd keep an eye on Dede and find out exactly why she'd picked *now* to introduce herself to Aunt Nan. When she had it all figured out, she'd tell Justin and Meghan and anyone else who cared to listen.

4

TO A TEE

"Maybe your Aunt Nan and Dede would give me some of their hair. One is white and one is almost black. They'd be fun to test," Meghan said as she and Elizabeth walked home from school.

"How many different kinds of hair are you going to test?" Elizabeth asked.

"As many as I can. I kind of wish I'd started this a little sooner."

"Did you ask about your blood type?"

Meghan clapped her hand over her mouth. "Forgot. But I will tonight—promise."

"Hey! You guys, wait up!" a voice called.

"It's Amy Catherine," said Meghan.

"*Don't* talk about the science fair," said Elizabeth.

"Hi," Amy Catherine said, pushing her glasses up on her nose. She stepped between Meghan and Elizabeth, forming the point of a pyramid with the two shorter girls on either side of her.

"How come you're walking?" Meghan asked.

"My mother had some kind of meeting this afternoon. It wouldn't be so bad if I didn't have all these books." Amy Catherine patted her bulging backpack.

"That's a lot of homework," said Elizabeth.

"No, research. For the science fair. Mom told me to check out all the books on," she paused, "my topic." Amy Catherine stopped and readjusted the pack.

"Oh," said Elizabeth. She wanted to look at Meghan, but she was afraid she'd laugh. So much for not talking about the science fair.

"Do either one of you know where I could get some colored electrical tape?" Amy Catherine asked.

"I don't. What about you, Elizabeth?" asked Meghan.

Colored electrical tape, Elizabeth thought. Could she use that to code the blood factors in her squares? Maybe wrap it around craft sticks? Colored sticks would be even better or … Elizabeth knew what would be perfect. Colored golf tees. Aunt Nan bought them by the bag.

"I guess Elizabeth doesn't know where to buy tape," said Amy Catherine.

"I'm sorry. You just gave me an idea," said Elizabeth.

"About electrical tape?" asked Amy Catherine.

"No, that won't work for me. I'll bet you could get it at a hardware store," said Elizabeth.

"So far we haven't found enough colors," Amy Catherine said. "Mom says it will be awfully hard to hand color all the wire, but we might have to do it."

And squares of wood with holes drilled in them to hold the golf tees, Elizabeth thought. She could almost see the entire project.

"I turn here," said Amy Catherine. She stopped and pushed her glasses up again. "My mother said I could have some people over after the science fair next Thursday. Do you think maybe you could come?"

"I'll have to ask," said Elizabeth. "It's a school night and I have a dance class."

"Me too," said Meghan.

Amy Catherine nodded, then cleared her throat. "Sure, okay." She turned the corner.

"Hey, Amy Catherine!" yelled Elizabeth.

The tall girl stopped but didn't look back.

"Thanks for your help."

Amy Catherine shrugged and continued on.

"She wins every year," said Meghan.

"Not *this* year," Elizabeth said.

"Are you even going to ask if you can go to her house?" asked Meghan.

"Yeah, I am. Amy Catherine is kind of different, and when I'm around her it makes me, I don't know, try harder or think more or something."

"You mean she makes you want to beat the pants off her?"

"Sort of." They giggled.

"Amy Catherine doesn't have a lot of friends. It would be awful to lose at the science fair *and* have no one show up at your party," said Elizabeth.

And I sort of like her, she thought, surprising herself.

"Can you stop by the house for awhile?" Meghan asked when they reached her corner. "I think there's some cake left over from last night. If you don't come and help me, I'll eat it all."

"I can't. I want to see what's up with Aunt Nan."

"Let me know anything interesting," said Meghan.

"See you tomorrow."

"Wow!" Meghan pointed at the truck pulling a long camper that had stopped at the intersection. "Wouldn't it be great to have one of those? They have everything—TVs, bathrooms, refrigerators. And you can take it anyplace—to the mountains, to the ocean, to Disneyland."

"Maybe you could ask for one for Christmas," said Elizabeth.

"I think I'll wait for my 16th birthday," said Meghan.

As she crossed the street in front of the RV, Elizabeth looked at the driver, expecting to see an older man or woman. To her surprise, a young man sat behind the wheel. He had long, dark hair and wore a brown cowboy hat with a silver-and-turquoise band around the crown. Elizabeth could have sworn that he was watching her as she crossed the street. She walked a little faster.

Neither Mike nor her mother was at home when Elizabeth arrived. Mike usually came home about a half hour after she did and Mom a few minutes after him. Mom taught language arts at Elizabeth's school, but she often stayed for meetings or to get ready for the next day.

Elizabeth decided she'd ask Aunt Nan for some golf tees. She needed them first, to know what size holes to drill in her squares.

Elizabeth grabbed the mail, then dumped it and her books on the chair beside the front door. She went outside and crossed the porch to Aunt Nan's.

As she pushed Aunt Nan's door open, she called out her name.

Dede came hurrying out of the kitchen. "*SHH!*" She touched her finger to her lips. "Don't you *ever* knock?" she asked in a low, angry voice. "Don't you have any manners?"

Elizabeth backed up one step, then another. Hot tears burned her eyes. She swallowed hard. It was like being told to get out of her own house. "Where's Aunt Nan?" Elizabeth finally managed to ask.

"She isn't feeling well so I put her to bed." Dede stood in front of Elizabeth, her arms crossed, almost like she was barring Elizabeth from the house.

"What's wrong with her?" Elizabeth asked, concern for Aunt Nan replacing her hurt feelings at Dede's harsh words.

"She must have a touch of the flu. Her stomach is hurting."

"Dede, did I hear Elizabeth come in?" Aunt Nan called from the bedroom.

Her voice sounded weak and shaky to Elizabeth.

"Now see what you did!" Dede said to Elizabeth through clenched teeth.

"It is indeed Elizabeth," Dede sang out to Aunt Nan in a completely different tone of voice.

Elizabeth pushed past Dede and went to Aunt Nan's bedroom. The shades were drawn making the normally bright room dim and shadowy.

"Are you all right?" Elizabeth asked, kneeling beside the bed.

"I will be," said Aunt Nan. She had on a yellow gown and her hair was uncombed. Elizabeth had never seen Aunt Nan look messy before.

"Can I do something? Get you something? Call Mom?" Elizabeth asked.

"I'd like a drink of water, I think. Dede's

been making me drink this herbal tea all day."
Aunt Nan handed Elizabeth a cup. Elizabeth
caught a whiff of the brown liquid left in the bottom. She thought she might have a stomachache
too if she had to drink that awful stuff.

"Why didn't you say you wanted some
water, Auntie?" asked Dede. "I'll get a glass for
you."

"Have I been asleep? How long?" asked
Aunt Nan, rubbing her hand over her face, then
closing her eyes again.

"You took a little nap, that's all. Are you
hungry?" Dede asked, using a singsong voice
like someone would use with a baby.

"No," said Aunt Nan. "I don't think I could
keep anything down."

"Are you all right?" Elizabeth took one of
Aunt Nan's hands and held it.

"Just tired," said Aunt Nan.

Dede tapped Elizabeth on the shoulder and
motioned her to follow. Elizabeth shook her
head. As she knelt beside the bed, she prayed for
Aunt Nan to get better. She felt her aunt's hand
on her head.

"You're such a sweet child," Aunt Nan murmured. She closed her eyes again.

Dede grabbed Elizabeth's arm and pulled her up, then pushed her toward the bedroom door.

"I'm calling my mother," said Elizabeth when they reached the living room.

"I think it would be a better idea to call a doctor," said Dede. "And *I'll* take care of that." She opened the front door.

Elizabeth didn't want to go and leave Aunt Nan alone with Dede, but she knew the best thing she could do for her aunt was to get her mother.

As she walked past Dede, Elizabeth paused and opened her mouth to speak. The words caught in her throat. Dede was wearing Aunt Nan's diamond-and-sapphire earrings.

5

THE DOCTOR IS A HE?

Elizabeth heard the door shut behind her, then the click of the lock. She waited on the porch, watching for her mother. To her surprise, a camper, like she and Meghan had seen earlier, drove into sight. As it approached the duplex, the RV seemed to slow down then speed up, passing by so quickly Elizabeth wasn't sure if it was the same man driving or not.

Bowing her head, Elizabeth prayed silently, Please, God, please make Aunt Nan all right. Surely God would help Aunt Nan. She was one of His biggest supporters. It was Aunt Nan who had dragged them back to church after Dad died and helped them find comfort in the fact that Jesus gave His life and rose again so Dad—and they—could live forever too.

Mom pulled the car into the driveway,

honked once, and waved at Elizabeth. "Is Mike home yet?" she asked as she climbed out of the car.

Elizabeth met her mother at the bottom of the porch steps and took one of her bags. "Something's wrong with Aunt Nan," she said. "You should see her. She's pale and her voice is weak. She's still wearing her nightgown."

Frowning, Mom opened the door to their side of the duplex. "But she's up?"

Elizabeth shook her head. "She was asleep when I went over, but she woke up and talked for a minute or two, then she drifted off again." Elizabeth felt the clutch of worry all over again. Aunt Nan was so full of life, always on the move, always doing something. To see her so still was scary.

"Is Dede with her?" asked Mom.

Elizabeth nodded. "She's giving her some disgusting herbal tea."

"Have they called the doctor?"

"Not yet. Won't you go check on her, please?" Elizabeth pleaded.

"Of course I'm going to check on her," Mom answered. "Is tonight Mike's Scout night?" She checked the calendar. "It is. That's why he's not home yet." She pulled a casserole out of the freezer and stuck it in the oven.

"Let's go. C'mon," said Mom.

Chewing on her thumbnail, Elizabeth followed her mother across the porch.

Mom opened the screen and turned the knob of the inside front door. It wouldn't open. "Dede must be a little more cautious than the rest of us," said Mom. She rapped sharply on the glass.

"Hi, Mrs. Bryan," Dede said, smiling brightly.

"Elizabeth said Nan is ill. What's wrong with her?" Mom asked as she stepped inside.

Once again, Dede stood between them and Aunt Nan. She positioned herself so Mom had to stand in the doorway or push Dede out of the way.

"Stomach flu, most likely," said Dede. "She keeps complaining about her stomach hurting and she's felt nauseous most of the day."

"Did you call the doctor?" Mom asked.

"I've been trying all day, and he just called me back. Said to keep on doing what I was doing—liquids and bed rest. If she isn't better tomorrow, call back."

"He? Dr. Havers wasn't there?" Mom asked.

Dede's eyes widened, and she took a step backward, like she was surprised by Mom's question.

Mom continued, "Did you ask him if this could possibly have something to do with Nan's ulcer? Did Nan say anything about her ulcer?"

Taking yet another step back, Dede looked at the floor and didn't answer. However, she gave Mom and Elizabeth enough room to get completely inside the house.

"And what about this herbal tea you've been giving her? Sometimes Nan has strange reactions to new foods." Mom started walking toward the bedroom.

Dede's head snapped up. "She's sleeping."

"I'd feel better if I could see her," Mom said, disappearing down the hallway leading to the bedrooms. Dede quickly followed.

Elizabeth sat down on the couch, content to let Mom see to Aunt Nan. She remembered the golf tees she'd come over to get in the first place. She was sure Aunt Nan wouldn't mind if she borrowed a few.

Elizabeth knew Aunt Nan stored her golf

bag in the living room coat closet. She'd put it away for her dozens of times after Aunt Nan returned from playing golf. She opened the closet door and pulled the golf bag out. In one of the pockets she found a few golf tees but not nearly enough. It was as bad as Mom's bag that never had any tees at all. Mom always relied on Aunt Nan to have extras.

Reaching up, Elizabeth felt along the shelf for a bag that might contain extra tees. As she patted her hand along, she came to a wallet. Elizabeth pulled it toward her. Recognizing it as Aunt Nan's, she wondered what it was doing out of her purse. On closer inspection, Elizabeth decided Aunt Nan must have gotten a new wallet. This one was nearly empty—the checkbook was gone and all her credit cards, even her driver's license. Elizabeth tossed the wallet back and continued her search for golf tees.

"What are you doing?" Dede practically screeched.

Elizabeth turned suddenly, and the sack she'd just found tipped, showering her with the golf tees she'd been looking for. Elizabeth dropped to her knees and started picking them up. "I needed some colored golf tees for a school project and knew Aunt Nan wouldn't mind if I used some of hers," Elizabeth explained.

"Of course she won't mind," Mom said as she came up behind them.

"Elizabeth is so sweet to be so concerned about my auntie," Dede said to Mom.

"We love Nan as if she were ours," Mom said. "If you need anything, if *Nan* needs anything, you let me know."

"I'm sure she'll feel much better in the morning," Dede said.

"I hope so. Elizabeth? Do you have what you need?"

Nodding, Elizabeth clutched the paper bag containing the golf tees. Dede stared at the bag, then lifted her eyes to Elizabeth's face. As Elizabeth scooted past her, Dede reached out and patted her on the arm, smiling.

Elizabeth wondered how dumb Dede thought she was. The smile looked like she'd cut it out of a circus poster and pasted it on. Elizabeth looked away, then back quickly.

Dede had taken Aunt Nan's earrings off and replaced them with long silver wires that had turquoise beads strung on them.

6

WHAT'S GOING ON NEXT DOOR?

"Are you sure we shouldn't be next door with Aunt Nan?" Elizabeth asked Mom.

"There's nothing we could do that Dede hasn't already done. Aunt Nan is sleeping and that's probably the best thing for her." Mom didn't look as sure as Elizabeth wanted her to look.

"You're worried about something," said Elizabeth.

"The doctor," said Mom. "Dr. Havers is a she not a he, and Dede never did explain why she talked to a different doctor. Maybe I should call." Mom checked the list of phone numbers posted by the telephone and dialed.

"Dr. Havers, please," Mom said. She listened for awhile.

"This is Lydia Bryan, and I'm not a patient, but my neighbor Nan Albright is. She isn't feeling well." Mom listened again. "Did someone else call today? About Nan? I see. Thank you. I'll call back tomorrow." Mom hung up.

"It's Dr. Havers' day off," she said. "The receptionist doesn't remember if anyone called about Nan or not. I'm sure Dede never expected to have to take care of a sick woman when she decided to visit. It's sweet of her to stay."

Sweet was not a word Elizabeth would have chosen to describe Dede.

"May I go to the basement and work on my science fair project? We have some wood scraps and a drill, don't we?"

"A drill? We have that old one. It's not electric or anything. It's one of those twisty kinds. Maybe I should come down and help you," said Mom.

"I can handle the drill by myself, and I promise not to drill through any body parts. I'll leave the door open and call you if I need help," said Elizabeth.

"You wouldn't consider letting Don help you, would you?" Mom asked.

"No," Elizabeth answered. Mom didn't

press. She seemed to understand Elizabeth's reluctance to accept Don Hamilton.

In the basement, Elizabeth found four squares of wood in the scrap box. All were approximately the same size. The workbench, tools, and wood scraps had been her dad's. Mom had left everything just the way it had been when Dad died. They used the tools occasionally but always put them back in the same place.

Elizabeth drew a light pencil cross dividing each wood square into four smaller squares. After marking the center, she drilled two holes about a half inch apart in the center of each smaller square.

She was so intent on her work, it was a few minutes before Elizabeth questioned the scraping noises she heard. When they finally penetrated her concentration, Elizabeth stopped and listened carefully.

Dad's workbench was against the wall between their side of the basement and Aunt Nan's. Elizabeth again heard something moving on the other side of the wall.

It had to be Dede. But what was she doing in the basement? Aunt Nan's washer and dryer were in a small utility room off the kitchen.

A snatch of a whisper drifted through. Elizabeth held her breath. She heard a low grunt and a prolonged scraping, like a lot of effort was being put into moving something heavy. When the scraping stopped, Elizabeth heard more whispering. She was sure there were two people in Aunt Nan's basement.

"Hey! Can I help?"

Elizabeth jumped, startled at her brother's arrival in the basement.

"I'm almost done. Go back upstairs and help Mom with dinner."

"She said to help you," Mike said.

Elizabeth quickly drilled the last two holes. She handed the square to her brother. "Take this upstairs."

"That's no fair. I wanted to drill," said Mike, sticking out his lower lip.

"You're too late." Elizabeth hung the drill on the pegboard, then started sweeping up.

Mike stomped up the stairs, then slammed the door shut.

Elizabeth stayed very still, listening for any sound from the other side of the basement. The only thing she heard was her own breathing.

Elizabeth picked through some colored wire, then carried it and the remaining wood squares up the stairs.

"Dinner's almost ready," Mom said as Elizabeth came out of the basement. "How did it go?"

"I'll show you after we eat," said Elizabeth.

"Could you show me now?" Mom asked.

"I need to do a few more things first," said Elizabeth.

"Honey, Don is coming over in a little while."

"Fine," said Elizabeth. "You can see it some other time." Mr. Hamilton was always at their house! And now she couldn't even go to Aunt Nan's to get away from him.

7

THE BLOOD
OF A FATHER

"Why do I need all this stuff for a science fair project?" Justin asked.

Elizabeth and Justin squeezed through crowded aisles at the hobby and art-supply store. To Elizabeth, it always seemed like she saw more people at the store looking at what it takes to make a science fair project than she ever saw at school viewing the finished projects.

"Here's poster board," said Justin, stopping in front of a rack that held a rainbow of colors.

"Not this kind. The foam board stands up a lot better," Elizabeth said, pointing at a different rack.

Justin picked up a sheet of foam board. "This stuff is expensive. It's going to clean me out to buy this and markers."

"You said it, man." A short, dark-haired boy

stuck the poster board he'd been holding back into the rack. "This is three day's lunch money."

"Hey, Rich," Justin said.

Elizabeth smiled but said nothing. Rich had joined their class at the beginning of the quarter, and she didn't know him very well. He sat in the back of the room and seldom spoke.

"Did you have to do a science project at your old school?" Justin asked.

Rich gave a short laugh. "No way. I can't imagine the old gang going for something like this. I'm thinking about using a cardboard box and saying I'm saving a tree." Rich shook his head and his long hair fell across his eyes. He jerked his head sideways and managed to move it off his forehead. Elizabeth wasn't sure how he did it.

"Everybody uses this stuff?" Rich nodded at the foam board.

"Some people use that stuff over there." Elizabeth pointed to a three-sided display box made specially for science fair projects.

"This is a weird, new world to me," said Rich. He stuck his hands in his jeans pockets. "Some of these parents seem more excited than the kids. I thought Mrs. Harms said that parents weren't supposed to do the projects. Mine don't have time, even if they felt like it."

"They're not supposed to help," said Elizabeth, "but you'll see. Some people don't exactly pay attention to that part of the instructions."

"I think I'll check out a few other stores and see what's happening there. Later." Rich turned and pushed through the crowd to the door.

"His dad is laid off from his job," explained Justin. "Rich is trying to get a paper route, but one hasn't opened up yet. I feel kind of sorry for him. He might not have the money for all this stuff."

Elizabeth nodded, feeling sorry for Rich too. Even though no special supplies were formally required, everybody used the same things. And it could cost a lot of money to make a display that fit in with the others at the science fair.

"Are you getting anything?" Justin asked.

"I've got some stuff left over from last year," said Elizabeth.

"Lucky you." Justin took his foam board and markers to the counter and joined the line.

Elizabeth wandered over to the window and watched the people walking by. A small park with benches and a fountain was directly across from the row of shops. She noticed a dog sitting on the end of one of the benches, beside a man and a woman. It looked so cute, just like a third person sitting there.

"I was going to ask if you wanted to have a soda or something, but I don't think I can afford one after this." Justin held out his purchases.

"We can get something at my house," said Elizabeth. "I'll show you my project."

"By the way, I found out my blood type," said Justin.

"Good. Look over in the park, at that dog. It's sitting there like a person."

"You need a dog to keep those two cats of yours company."

"I don't think so." Elizabeth held the door open so Justin could get through with his bulky pieces of foam board. She looked at the dog again just in time to see it jump over the back of the bench and take off after a squirrel. The woman stood up, turned around, and yelled at the dog.

Elizabeth was so surprised to recognize the woman that she let go of the door and practically knocked Justin back into the store.

"Hey, my hands are kinda full here," Justin said.

Elizabeth grabbed Justin and pushed him in front of her. She peeked over his shoulder, still watching the woman in the park.

"What are you doing?" Justin asked.

"I don't want her to see me," explained Elizabeth. The man and the woman had finally caught the dog and were trying to get him to sit again. "That's Dede. Aunt Nan's Dede. But who is the guy? And where'd the dog come from?"

"I don't even understand where Dede came from," said Justin.

Dede and the man talked for a few more minutes, then they leaned toward one another and kissed.

"They must know each other," said Justin.

"But she's from New Mexico and she came on a bus. Do they let dogs on buses?"

The man started to walk away, but the dog kept trying to get back to Dede.

"Maybe she isn't so bad. The dog seems to like her a lot," Justin said.

Dede gave the dog a hug, then pointed to the man. The dog turned around and barked once at Dede, then followed the man.

"*Who* would she know here?" Elizabeth asked. "Wait a minute and see where she goes."

Dede opened the leather backpack she had slung over her shoulder and poked around inside for awhile. She pulled something out and stuck it in the pocket of her denim jacket, then started walking away from Elizabeth and Justin.

"That's not the way to Aunt Nan's," said Elizabeth.

"Maybe she's running errands. The drug store is that direction. And the bank," said Justin.

"It doesn't seem strange to you that she's kissing some guy?"

"Sort of," said Justin. "Maybe he's one lucky guy." He smiled at Elizabeth.

She felt her cheeks warm and wished she didn't blush so easily. "Let's go on home. Aunt Nan may be all alone. Maybe I can talk to her about Dede," said Elizabeth.

All the way home Elizabeth tried to figure out who it was Dede had met in the park. It didn't feel right to her.

As they approached the house, Justin asked, "Have you solved all the mysteries yet, Sherlock?"

"Not yet," Elizabeth answered, "but I'm working on it."

"You never give up, do you?"

"Nope," said Elizabeth. "I wonder where Mom is? There's no car in the drive."

The front door was unlocked. As soon as she opened it, Elizabeth heard Mr. Hamilton's voice. She looked at the street and saw his car parked at the curb. She must really be distracted by Dede to miss that car.

"Mr. Hamilton's here!" A smile spread across Justin's face. Mr. Hamilton had been the baseball coach of Mike's team last summer. Justin had helped with the team. Elizabeth counted Justin among Mr. Hamilton's fans.

"Where's Mom?" Elizabeth directed the question to Mike.

"She and Aunt Nan went shopping, so Mr. *Hamburger* is baby-sitting me." Mike giggled when he called Mr. Hamilton, Mr. Hamburger.

"Mr. Hamburger!" Mr. Hamilton tickled Mike to the ground.

"You called me *Hotdog*," Mike shrieked through his laughter.

"You are a little hotdog," said Justin, teasing, "out there on your in-line skates, jumping curbs, skating backward. I've seen you."

"You're a pepperoni pizza," Mike said to

Justin. Mr. Hamilton had quit tickling him so Mike jumped on the man's back and hung there.

Elizabeth went to the kitchen and poured herself and Justin a glass of apple juice, then checked the cookie jar. There were still a few oatmeal cookies so she put them on a plate next to the glasses.

When she walked through the living room to get her science project, Justin was deep in conversation with Mr. Hamilton. The names they were discussing were unfamiliar to Elizabeth so she figured they must be talking about sports.

Elizabeth carried her wooden squares and golf tees downstairs from her bedroom. "C'mon out to the kitchen when you're finished," she said.

Justin nodded and continued to talk.

Elizabeth had made red As, blue Bs, and white Os out of the colored wire. She'd marked the red golf tees with an A, the blue ones with a B, and the white ones with an O to represent each blood type. She sorted the colors and placed them in separate piles.

"Okay, I'm ready." Justin slid into a chair, took a big drink of juice and ate a cookie in two bites.

"What's your blood type?" Elizabeth asked.

"It's O positive."

"Did you find out your parents' types?" Elizabeth asked.

"Mom is A positive and Dad is O positive."

"Okay." Elizabeth chose a wood block and laid it on the table in front of her. She took two white-wire Os and put one above each of the top squares. She picked up a red-wire A and laid it next to the top left square. She placed white golf tees in one of the holes drilled in the center of each of the smaller squares. Then she put red golf tees in each of the second holes in the row next to the red-wire A.

"There are only four possible blood types— A, B, AB, and O," Elizabeth explained as she pointed to the different wire letters. "Each parent contributes one chromosome to determine the blood type of their child. The O chromosome is recessive, which means to be an O blood type, both chromosomes have to be O. You only got Os from your dad." Elizabeth pointed at all the white golf tees.

"So how come I'm O and not A?" Justin asked.

"You could have been A. But your mom

must have gotten an A and an O chromosome from her parents. It's the only way you could end up with a blood type of O." Elizabeth stopped and placed a wire O next to the bottom left square and added white golf tees to the remaining empty holes.

"You had a 50-50 chance of being a type A because the A and B chromosomes dominate when they pair with an O chromosome. So for you to be type O, your Mom had to be AO and your Dad OO.

"If your mom was type AA," Elizabeth took away the wire O and one white golf tee from each of the squares of the bottom row and replaced them with an A and red tees, "you would have had type A blood."

"Let me do one." Justin pulled a wooden square over.

"Okay, the mother has type A and the father has type B," Elizabeth said. "Their child has type O."

Justin put a red A above one of the squares and a blue B next to the top row. He put a red A golf tee and a blue B golf tee in the upper left square. "Wait a minute, the kid is O, but neither parent has an O chromosome."

"Look at yours," suggested Elizabeth.

"Oh, there has to be one square with two Os in it," Justin said as he put two white tees in the lower right square.

"Now work backward," said Elizabeth.

Justin picked up two wire Os. He put one next to the A and the other under the B. He put one white golf tee in each of the empty squares, added a blue one in the top right and a red one in the bottom left square. "Wow," he said, "this kid could have been any blood type."

"A and B are codominant," said Elizabeth, "so that's where the fourth blood type comes from."

"That's a terrific project," said Mr. Hamilton.

Elizabeth's head jerked up. She hadn't noticed when he came in.

"What's your blood type?" Justin asked Elizabeth.

"My family is really neat," she said. "We all have a different type." She quickly filled in a square.

"My dad," Elizabeth glanced up at Mr. Hamilton, "was AB. My mom is O. I'm A and Mike is B."

"I'm O too, like your Mom," said Mr. Hamilton. He filled out the fourth wooden square with all white wires and tees.

"Then you could never be my father," Elizabeth said. She realized immediately what she had said and glanced at Mr. Hamilton to see his reaction. She quickly looked away, wishing she could take her words back. The look on Mr. Hamilton's face—his eyes and mouth forming large dark ohs of surprise and pain—had an unwelcome effect on her.

Silence grew until it seemed like a fourth presence. Elizabeth thought if she reached up she'd be able to feel it building a wall between her and Mr. Hamilton.

Finally, Mr. Hamilton cleared his throat. "You've certainly worked hard on the project. It's going to be a big success." He turned and disappeared into the shadows of the living room.

Elizabeth quickly took apart the square Mr. Hamilton had assembled. When the white Os and golf tees were returned to their piles, she dared to look at Justin.

He raised his eyebrows and opened his mouth.

"Don't say anything. I feel bad enough already," Elizabeth admitted in a low voice. She had no idea what to do next—apologize, pretend the whole thing never happened, tell Mom. Please God, she breathed, what do I do now?

"Elizabeth?"

Justin's voice jarred her. She opened her eyes.

"What are you doing?" he asked.

"I'm asking God to help me. I feel so bad. I know I really did it this time."

Mr. Hamilton stuck his head through the door. "Since you're here to watch Mike, I think I'll push off. Tell your mom I'll talk to her later."

Elizabeth had a moment of panic. She looked at Justin, hoping he'd tell her what to do, but he said nothing.

Mr. Hamilton gave a wave, and Elizabeth heard the front door shut. Mike came into the kitchen and climbed into the chair between Justin and Elizabeth.

Pushing away from the table, Elizabeth followed Mr. Hamilton. As she stepped out onto the porch, he pulled his car away from the curb.

Had God finally answered her prayer? It didn't feel that way at all.

8

PICTURES
DON'T LIE

"Don't you have anything to do besides stand on the porch?" Elizabeth heard Dede before she saw her coming up the walk.

Still reeling from the incident with Mr. Hamilton, Elizabeth didn't answer.

Dede dropped her bulging backpack at Elizabeth's feet, then stretched her arms over her head.

"What's in there?" Elizabeth asked, pointing at the backpack. It wasn't nearly that full the last time she'd seen it.

"Books, heavy books. You have a pretty good library for a little town on the prairie."

If someone else had said it, Elizabeth might have found it funny. "St. Louis is one of the biggest cities in the country."

"Big, yes." Dede dragged the pack of books

across the porch to Aunt Nan's door. "Is she back yet?"

"Not yet." Elizabeth sighed. What was she going to tell Mom about Mr. Hamilton? She turned to go inside but stopped when she felt Dede staring at her.

"What?" Elizabeth asked.

Dede shrugged and unlocked the door.

Justin came out of Elizabeth's house, carrying his foam board. "I think I'd better get home," he said.

"Well, well, well," said Dede. "Entertaining the boyfriend when Mom's not at home? And quite a good-looking one I might add." The young woman smiled broadly at Justin.

Justin's face reddened in the shadow of the bill of his baseball cap.

"This is Dede," Elizabeth said.

"And you are?" Dede held out her hand.

"Justin," he answered, mumbling. He gave Dede's hand a short shake.

"*Very* pleased to meet you." A smile played at the corners of Dede's mouth. Her eyes darted back and forth between Elizabeth and Justin.

Elizabeth realized Dede was enjoying making them uncomfortable.

Mom's car pulled into the drive.

The sly smile disappeared, and Dede donned what Elizabeth decided to call a "mask of concern." She'd read that somewhere and it described exactly the expression Dede always wore when Aunt Nan was around.

Dede met Aunt Nan at the bottom of the steps and held her arm to help her climb the steps—like Aunt Nan was an old lady or something. Elizabeth didn't think Aunt Nan would like that much.

"It was good to get out of the house," Aunt Nan said.

Elizabeth gave Aunt Nan a kiss on the cheek. Aunt Nan hugged her in return.

"Hello, Justin," she said.

"Hi, Mrs. Albright. I'm glad you're feeling better," Justin said.

"Thank you, dear. It was a nasty old flu bug. I hope none of the rest of you get it."

"Come on and I'll fix you a nice cup of tea." Dede put her arm around Aunt Nan and turned her away from Elizabeth.

"Lydia has supper planned for us, Dede." Aunt Nan turned back.

"Hi, sweetie," Mom said to Elizabeth as she

walked up the steps, her arms loaded with grocery bags.

Justin propped his foam board against the wall of the house and grabbed several of the bags. Elizabeth took the rest. "Thanks." Mom smiled. "Where's Don?"

Elizabeth's stomach dropped. "He ... he ... he had to go," she stammered.

"That's odd." Mom's forehead wrinkled, then she shrugged. "C'mon in. I'm making some baked potatoes with all the fixings." She held the door open.

Elizabeth and Justin carried the grocery bags to the kitchen. Elizabeth's project was still spread on the table, so they lined the bags up on the counter, and Mom started unpacking.

"Nan, you stretch out on the couch," she called over her shoulder. Mom pulled out a small white pharmacy bag and ripped it open. She filled a glass with water and shook a tablet from the bottle into her hand. "Take this to Aunt Nan," Mom said, handing the pill and glass to Elizabeth.

"Why? What's wrong with her?" Elizabeth asked.

"She's a little stressed, you know, Dede

showing up out of the blue, and that flu took it out of her. The doctor didn't want her ulcer acting up again so she prescribed some medicine."

Justin followed Elizabeth into the living room.

"I hate pills," Aunt Nan crabbed, wrinkling her nose.

"Gotta go," Justin said again.

"See you Monday," Elizabeth said.

"Bye, Justin," Dede said, wiggling her fingers in a wave.

"Bye," he said.

"Elizabeth, run next door and get that photo album off the top shelf of the closet in the upstairs bedroom. The one with the brown cover and all the old pictures."

"Upstairs bedroom? You mean my room?" Dede asked, frowning.

"I said upstairs," Aunt Nan replied.

"I'll get it or it can wait. You don't have to bother showing me the pictures now," said Dede.

"I told you I'd remember someday and I remember now. Go on, Lizzybeth. You know exactly where I'm talking about," said Aunt Nan.

Elizabeth felt a thrill of excitement. She was

going to get to see Dede's room. And know the layout? She knew it as well as her own room. It was a mirror image.

She grabbed the key to Aunt Nan's house from the rack in the front closet and went next door. The house was already unlocked. Elizabeth remembered Dede had taken a key out of her backpack right before Aunt Nan came home. And the backpack still lay by the door. She dragged it inside, wondering what kind of books Dede had checked out. The bag weighed a ton!

Unable to resist, Elizabeth opened the flap on the bag and peeked inside. She didn't know what she'd expected, but it wasn't the art books she found. The pictures on the covers were of desert scenes, cactus, and sunsets. Boring! Elizabeth ran upstairs.

The bedroom looked much the same as it always had. The bed was neatly made, and there were no clothes on the floor. Elizabeth opened the closet. The picture album was exactly where Aunt Nan had said it would be.

When Elizabeth pulled it down, several sheets of paper fluttered to the floor. She gathered the loose pages, wondering if they belonged inside the album or on the shelf. They were sketches of a river scene. Elizabeth stuck them inside the album.

Dede's few clothes hung in the corner of the closet. Her navy blue canvas duffle rested on the floor, unzipped, but the edges overlapping. Elizabeth tried but couldn't see inside it. She nudged the bag with her toes, hoping it might fall open. It didn't work.

At first glance, Elizabeth thought nothing of the initials on the bag. She turned to leave, then paused and looked back at the bag. Returning to the closet, she knelt, leaning over the bag: *SJC.*

Elizabeth heard a creak, like someone coming up the stairs. She jumped, hitting the clothes hanging above her head and causing the hangers to clatter noisily against the metal bar. No one appeared at the top of the steps, but Elizabeth felt uneasy. She stayed perfectly quiet but heard nothing.

Elizabeth tiptoed to the stairwell and peered cautiously over the edge. Nothing. At her house, the strange noises usually ended up being the cats, but Aunt Nan didn't have any pets. She went downstairs, still on guard.

If she questioned Dede about having a bag

with completely different initials, Elizabeth knew what people would say. Of course she borrowed it from SJC. She could mention it to Justin now that he'd met Dede. Elizabeth was pretty sure he wasn't one of Dede's fans.

Aunt Nan had her eyes closed when Elizabeth returned. She sat down beside her quietly, wondering what had happened to Dede.

"Did you find it?" Aunt Nan asked. "Where's Dede gone to now?"

"Is this the album?" Elizabeth asked. As she handed it to Aunt Nan, the sketches fell out.

"What are these?" Aunt Nan asked.

"They were either in the album or on the closet shelf," Elizabeth said.

As Aunt Nan looked at the three drawings, Elizabeth looked too. "Could be Dede's. Turns out she's an artist."

That explained the art books, Elizabeth thought, but not the creak from the stairs. Where was Dede?

"I had a little oil painting. I got it out in New Mexico when I visited Helen the last time. It was this same type of scene, a river behind a cabin."

"Dinner will be ready in a minute." Dede came in from the kitchen, disappointing Elizabeth. She was sure she'd been spying on her at Aunt Nan's. Maybe her imagination was running away with her.

"Dede, did you draw these?" Aunt Nan held up the sketches.

Dede glanced at the pages.

"Are these yours?" Aunt Nan asked again.

"Just scribbles," Dede said, taking the sketches, folding them and stuffing them in her pocket. "You talked like you missed that painting, and I thought I might try to do something similar for you."

Aunt Nan shook her head. "I wish I could remember what I did with it. I read an article in the *New York Times* about the artist who painted it. He's gotten very famous, and the price I paid would be considered a bargain. I tried to find the picture after I read the article, but I couldn't. Wonder if I sold it at a garage sale?"

Elizabeth watched Dede. The woman was listening hard to Aunt Nan, drinking in every word she said.

"By the way, Lizzybeth, Dede said she'd help if you need any artwork for your science fair project," said Aunt Nan.

"Sure, I'd love to," Dede added.

And Dede *looked* ready and eager to do it. But she sounded the same. Elizabeth wondered what would happen if she actually took her up on the offer. She figured it would be bye-bye science fair project.

"No thanks. I've got it under control," Elizabeth said, her eyes still on Dede, who couldn't be nicer now that they were with Aunt Nan.

Dede shrugged and even managed to look hurt at Elizabeth's refusal of her offer to help. "If you change your mind."

Aunt Nan opened the photo album. The first pictures were of a young Aunt Nan and another woman who looked remarkably like her. "Your mom and me," she said to Dede.

Leaning closer, Dede stared at the pictures, her eyes glistening. "She was beautiful," Dede whispered.

"And so full of life, always smiling and joking," said Aunt Nan. "When she was sick, I wished there was some way they could drain all that sick blood out of her so I could give her some of mine. We matched, you know."

Elizabeth's ears perked up. They were talking in her territory now. It was just like her science fair project. "What type?" she asked.

"AB," said Aunt Nan. "Is that what you are?" she asked Dede.

Dede shrugged.

"You could be," said Elizabeth, "depending on what your dad was. The only thing you couldn't be is type O."

"How interesting," said Dede in a way that let Elizabeth know it wasn't at all.

Elizabeth concentrated on the pictures in the album as Aunt Nan slowly turned the pages.

"Do you remember my visit at all?" Aunt Nan asked. "I remember you and your little friend—Sasha wasn't it? The two of you were inseparable. Is she still around?" She pointed at a picture of two little girls, both dark-haired but one smiling and one looking very serious.

"Sasha? I haven't thought of her in years," said Dede.

In the next picture, the same little girls were standing on a log laid across a rushing stream. They were waving at the camera. On the next page, the girls were about to tumble off the log. In the next picture, the two of them stood in the shallow stream, soaked.

"She pushed me. I remember *that*," said Dede. "And the water was freezing!"

The final picture in the book was of the smiling girl and the young woman. The woman, stretched out in a lounge chair, had the girl wrapped in a striped towel and was hugging her close. The other girl stood to one side with a much smaller towel, drying herself.

Dede reached out and touched the woman's face. "My mom, right before she died. I remember now why you came to visit."

"The last time I saw either one of you," Aunt Nan said in a husky voice.

"You took me shopping for something to wear to the funeral, and we got a navy blue sailor dress. The only clothes I had were jeans and shorts."

As much as Elizabeth *didn't* want it to be true, at that moment it seemed like Dede truly was Aunt Nan's niece.

THE SCIENCE FAIR

The day dragged on and on, each teacher talking about something more boring than the last. Elizabeth couldn't think about anything but the science fair. Her project was finished and in Mom's car, waiting for her to set it up in the gym—as soon as school was over.

The final bell rang, and Elizabeth rushed to her locker. She stuffed her books inside and took out the markers, tape, and other supplies she'd brought with her.

At the car, Elizabeth had to wait for her mother. "Where *is* she?" she said to Justin and Meghan as they watched parents pull up and help their kids unload project after project.

"She'll be here," Justin said. He was busy double-checking all the pieces of his project.

Elizabeth tried the car door again.

"Look, there's Amy Catherine," said Meghan.

A blue minivan had pulled up beside the gym doors. Amy Catherine was pulling on the back doors almost before it stopped. Her mother got out and stopped Amy Catherine before she had the project out. The two of them talked, her mother gesturing, pointing, and shaking her head. Amy Catherine's shoulders slumped and her head dropped as her mother pushed her out of the way and removed a large plywood board covered in black plastic.

"What is that?" Meghan asked.

Amy Catherine followed her mother, carrying a large box.

"I hope I'm not next to her," said Elizabeth. "But I can't wait to see what her project is."

Mom came running across the parking lot. She unlocked the car and Elizabeth pulled her poster board out of the back seat. Justin held it while Elizabeth grabbed the box containing her wooden squares, wires, and golf tees.

"There's my mom!" said Meghan. "I can always count on her to miss the rush." She ran to the car and unloaded her project.

"I can come help," Meghan's mother said.

"It's *my* project," Meghan replied. "You helped by driving me around and bringing this stuff to school. Really, Mom, I'm fine."

Mom and Mrs. Harris stayed behind on the sidewalk while Elizabeth, Justin, and Meghan carried their projects inside.

"Do you still want to color your hair?" Elizabeth asked as they waited in line to get their assigned places.

"That stuff smells disgusting," Meghan answered. "The dye, I mean. And leave it on a little too long or use the wrong color and, well, my hair looks better boring brown. You'll see what I mean."

Elizabeth and Justin were assigned spots on the same bank of tables, but Meghan's number sent her to the other side of the gym.

When Elizabeth reached her spot, she saw Amy Catherine setting up on the opposite side of the table and one spot down. Amy Catherine's face was red, and she kept wiping her eyes as her mom arranged and rearranged the display.

Elizabeth took time to peek at Amy Catherine's project. It was a large map of the United States. Samples of something, Elizabeth couldn't tell what, were set out in front of the map. It looked like each one was attached to the map with colored wire. Amy Catherine had moved away from the table, leaning against the wall with her arms folded over her chest, while her mother fussed with the pieces of the project.

As Elizabeth set out her project, Mrs. Harms passed by. She stopped and picked up one of the squares, then read the poster. "Nice work," she said, smiling.

"Thanks," Elizabeth answered shyly.

Mrs. Harms patted Elizabeth on the arm and continued to the next student.

When she checked Amy Catherine's project again, Elizabeth was even happier she didn't have to exhibit next to her. The project had lights and buzzers in addition to everything else. She saw Rich walking down the aisle carrying a cardboard box and a backpack. He paused at the empty space behind Elizabeth and next to Amy Catherine, watching as Amy Catherine and her mother continued to add to the project.

As soon as Elizabeth finished, she went to see Justin's project. He wasn't there, but his project, displaying balls of every size and color, looked good. She decided to get a drink of water, then find Meghan. The two of them could tour the rest of the projects, checking out the competition. The gym would close soon and the judges would decide which projects won the blue ribbons that entitled them to go to the citywide science fair. The results would be announced at a ceremony later that evening. Elizabeth got butterflies in her stomach thinking about it.

Elizabeth heard the sound of ripping cardboard before she saw anything. In a corner, beside a trash can, Rich stood tearing and then throwing away pieces of the box he'd carried into the gym.

"Hey!" said Elizabeth. "Finish your recycling project?"

Rich turned his back on Elizabeth, but not before she got a glimpse of his eyes, red rimmed and wet. "This science fair business is a bunch of crap," he said in a low, hoarse voice.

"But you said you had a project."

"Yeah, right, a project." Rich threw the rest of the box away. "Bunch of kids bringing in stuff their rich moms and dads bought."

"That's not true," Elizabeth said.

"I'm glad I didn't waste my time. I was supposed to set up next to Princess Amy Catherine." Rich's voice dropped off and he sniffed loudly. He turned quickly, then backed up, staring over Elizabeth's shoulder.

She turned. Amy Catherine stood right behind her, tears streaming down her cheeks.

"I did too work on my project. My mom and dad helped, but they didn't do it all," Amy Catherine said. "My mom just doesn't want me to be embarrassed. She says you're all jealous of me, that's all." She straightened her shoulders and went into the girls' bathroom.

"Jealous," Rich said sarcastically, then walked away, leaving Elizabeth standing alone.

The cardboard box stuck out of the trash can beckoning Elizabeth. She pulled it out, and her heart sank to her toes as she read the "poster" Rich had drawn in black crayon. Underneath the pieces of cardboard she saw the trash he'd brought in to display in his recycling project. On the poster, Rich had detailed how long it took to get rid of different kinds of trash in different ways and the effect each had on the environment. She carried the remains to the gym door and searched the crowd for Mrs. Harms.

Elizabeth found Mrs. Harms at the same moment the teacher found Rich. Before she could reach them, Mrs. Harms took Rich by the arm, a serious look on her face.

"You promised you were working on a project," Mrs. Harms said. "This is inexcusable, and we *will* meet with the principal about it."

Rich pulled away and sprinted for the exit. Mrs. Harms watched him go, an angry frown replacing her usual smile.

"Where did Rich go?" Elizabeth asked.

Mrs. Harms shook her head and pressed her lips together.

"Mrs. Harms, he did a project."

The teacher turned to Elizabeth, her hand slowly rising to cover her mouth.

"I'm not sure what happened, but he was supposed to set up next to Amy Catherine. This is his project, at least what's left of it." Elizabeth held out the box. "We saw him at the art-supply store looking at poster board, but it was so expensive. I think maybe he didn't want to set this up with all the other projects."

Mrs. Harms took the box and looked down at it, her eyes filling with tears. She chewed on her lower lip. "Those things I said to him when he was already hurting. How can I …" her voice trailed off.

"It'll be okay," Elizabeth said, but she wasn't sure about that. She could imagine what Rich must have felt when he saw the shiny new poster board displays stretching from one end of the gym to the other, not to mention the lighted displays and the computer-drawn graphs and tables. Mrs. Harms had stressed over and over that students were to do the work themselves, using materials they had at home. One of the problems was that some homes had a lot more materials than others.

Mrs. Harms squared her shoulders. "This will *never* happen again. For years I've thought that working on the projects at school would give everyone a fair chance. Now I know I was right." She marched away.

Before she even had a chance to think about what Mrs. Harms had said, Elizabeth felt a hand on her arm.

"There you are! I'm so glad I finally found you," Mom said.

"My project is set up, but I haven't had a chance to look at ... Mom, what's wrong?"

"It's Aunt Nan. She's been in a car accident, and she's at the hospital."

10 THE RIGHT TYPE ...

Mom pulled Elizabeth close, and they clung to one another.

"But I thought ..." Elizabeth started her sentence. "She was ..." The thoughts were crowding in so quickly they wouldn't form into words. *What* was wrong? Was Aunt Nan going to—die? A large, cold lump lodged itself in Elizabeth's chest. She felt weak; she was glad Mom was holding onto her.

"Aunt Nan needs our prayers. God will see her through this," Mom said.

Elizabeth nodded, but she couldn't help remembering her father's last trip to the hospital. Mom had said the same thing then.

"Do you want to go with me to the hospital?"

Elizabeth nodded again.

"I don't think I can drive. I've called Don, and he's picking us up out front."

Even the mention of Mr. Hamilton didn't phase Elizabeth. All the noise and activity in the gym seemed far away and fuzzy as she concentrated all her energy on prayers for Aunt Nan.

"Hey, Elizabeth! Come see my project. You should see what I did to your hair." Meghan ran up to them, then stopped. "What's the matter?"

"Aunt Nan is in the hospital," Mom explained.

"No!" gasped Meghan. "She's going to be all right, isn't she?"

"Yes," said Elizabeth firmly. "She was in a car accident. We'll know more when we get to the hospital. I hope."

Meghan grabbed Elizabeth and gave her a quick hug. "I'll be praying for your Aunt Nan," she whispered, warming Elizabeth slightly.

"There's Don," said Mom, towing Elizabeth behind her to the car. As soon as they got in, Mom started explaining once again what had happened.

Elizabeth wished they knew more.

"You two go on inside," said Mr. Hamilton, stopping at the entrance to the emergency room.

"I'll pick up Mike, and we'll come back here. He's probably wondering where everyone is."

"I can't believe I forgot about Mike!" said Mom, her face turning even paler. "Nan was going to watch him until we got home."

"Where's Dede? Is she at the house?" asked Elizabeth.

"She's at the hospital too. She was in the car when it happened."

"She's hurt?" asked Elizabeth.

"Not as badly as Aunt Nan," said Mom. "I think she needed some stitches."

Mr. Hamilton leaned over and put his arm around Mom. "It'll be okay," he said softly.

Mom nodded. Mr. Hamilton kissed Mom and then held her for a few moments.

Elizabeth had thought she couldn't feel any worse after the news about Aunt Nan, but the exchange between Mr. Hamilton and her mother made the lump in her chest grow even bigger and colder. She got out of the car and slammed the door as hard as she could. She refused to sit and watch the two of them act like teenagers.

Mom caught up with her in the waiting area. When she tried to put her arm around Elizabeth, Elizabeth pulled away.

"There's Dede!" Mom said.

Dede had a bandage above one eye, but otherwise she looked fine. When Mom took her hand, Dede looked at her like she didn't recognize her.

"How's Nan?" Mom was asking as Elizabeth joined them.

"The doctors still haven't told me anything," Dede said. She touched the bandage.

"Is there anyone here named Lydia?" a nurse asked from between a pair of double doors that separated the treatment rooms from the waiting area.

"Me!" Mom answered.

"Could you come back here for a moment?" the nurse asked.

Dede started to follow Mom, but at the doors the nurse turned her away.

"What happened?" Elizabeth asked.

"A guy ran a stop sign and hit us. It was awful! The paramedics had to cut Aunt Nan out of the car. I thought I was blind. But there was just so much blood in my eyes I couldn't see."

"Was she still alive?" Elizabeth asked in little more than a whisper.

"She was alive and talking the whole time, telling them what to do. But she looked awful, gray and old. I could tell she was in a lot of pain," said Dede.

Elizabeth started chewing on her nails.

"Dede, Elizabeth, come on back here," Mom said.

The two girls couldn't move fast enough. Mom put her arm around Dede's shoulders. "We know now why God sent you to us when He did," she said, giving Dede a hug.

Dede pulled away and looked at Mom, puzzled.

"Nan is going to be all right the doctors say, but she needs an operation. The car accident caused some internal injuries and there's some bleeding. She needs a blood transfusion, and she said she thinks the two of you have the same blood type. Are you willing to be a donor?"

"Of course," said Dede.

"I will too," said Elizabeth.

Mom smiled at her, a tired smile. "Sweetie, we all would donate, but our blood wouldn't help much. Aunt Nan needs AB negative and that's a pretty rare type."

"She knows my blood type? I'm not even sure what my blood type is," said Dede.

"We were talking about it the other night.

Your mom and Aunt Nan had the same blood type," said Elizabeth, "but she didn't know what yours was. It really doesn't matter because AB is the universal recipient. She can have a transfusion of any kind of blood, but it has to be negative." Elizabeth realized she'd learned a lot from her science fair project. She certainly didn't think she'd have to be applying it to someone she knew so well.

"If she can have any type, then I guess I'm a match," said Dede.

"But it's better if we can give her a perfect match," the nurse said, smiling.

"Can we see Aunt Nan?" Elizabeth asked.

"Not until after the surgery," said Mom. "But I'm sure she's going to be all right. All the pieces are in place."

The nurse took Dede by the arm. "Come with me, and we'll do some tests. Then they'll draw the blood."

Dede followed her into a treatment room.

"What about us? What can we do to help Aunt Nan? Are you sure we can't see her?" asked Elizabeth.

Mom took Elizabeth's hand and moved toward a seat. "We can pray."

11

OR THE
WRONG TYPE?

Elizabeth hurt all over. It felt like they'd been sitting and praying and wondering for hours. Why didn't someone come and tell them what was happening with Aunt Nan?

"Mom!" Mike's voice filled the small hospital chapel as he ran to the pew.

Mom gave him a big hug. "Sh," she said.

"How's Nan?" Mr. Hamilton asked.

"In surgery," answered Mom.

Justin sat down beside Elizabeth.

"What are you doing here?" she asked, glad to see him.

"I stopped by your house on the way home to see if anybody knew anything about Mrs. Albright, and Mr. Hamilton said I could come along."

"Thanks," said Elizabeth.

"Why don't we all go to the cafeteria?" Mr. Hamilton asked.

Mom shook her head. "It's so peaceful here, and I want to keep praying for Nan."

"You've been praying all this time?" Justin asked.

"Whenever things are bad, we know that we can find some peace in Jesus' love," said Elizabeth, searching hard for the right words. She knew Justin wasn't comfortable with talk about religion. "Aunt Nan knows we're here too, so she'll feel stronger."

"I expected to find you chewing your nails and crying," said Justin. "I can't believe how calm you seem."

Elizabeth smiled. "I was chewing my nails, but Mom and I came in here and prayed. Jesus will take care of Aunt Nan."

A nurse opened the door. "Mrs. Bryan?"

Mom stood up.

"Do you know what happened to Mrs. Albright's niece?" the nurse asked.

"I thought she was giving blood," said Mom.

"We did a type and crossmatch and found out she isn't AB negative after all. The girl is O positive."

"But Nan was so sure …"

A picture of a Punnett square popped into Elizabeth's head, and she couldn't make it go away. Something that the nurse just said made her uneasy. Dede's mom was AB. That put an A or a B in every square. She couldn't be type O! There was no way. Either Aunt Nan didn't remember the types correctly or Dede wasn't her niece.

The nurse shrugged. "She was upset she couldn't help her aunt and left in a hurry. She left this behind. Could you keep it for her?" She handed Mom a bulging billfold.

"Nan is still in surgery?" Mom asked.

"They should be finished soon."

"Maybe Dede is up in the waiting area by the OR," said Mr. Hamilton. "Let's go see."

"You go ahead. I want to stay here a little longer."

"I'll go with you," Justin said.

"Me too," said Mike.

"Elizabeth, you can go," said Mom.

Elizabeth stayed right where she was. Dede wasn't Aunt Nan's niece. It was so perfectly clear—the telephone call, the initials. But how did Dede know so much about the family? And why was she here?

"Mom?"

Mom sighed and turned to Elizabeth.

"Dede couldn't have type O blood, not if her mother was AB."

"Elizabeth, this is neither the time nor the place for you to let your prejudices against Dede show. It's obvious when you don't like someone, whether it's Dede or Don. But I refuse to sit here in a church and listen to you try to drag poor Dede down. Not tonight when I have so much else to worry about." Mom turned away.

Elizabeth felt the cold lump grow bigger and harder. She knew it wouldn't do any good to say anything else to Mom. She left the room, hoping to find Dede and ask her what was going on.

Seeing the billfold lying on the pew, Elizabeth picked it up and took it with her.

Mr. Hamilton, Mike, and Justin were the only people in the waiting room. They were bent over an old issue of *Sports Illustrated*.

A doctor entered the area. "Is anyone here for Mrs. Albright?" he asked.

"We are." They rushed the doctor.

"She's a remarkable woman," he said. "And she'll be just fine. She asked if she could just have a local to make sure we did the procedure correctly!" He chuckled.

Sounds like Aunt Nan, Elizabeth thought.

"We've stopped the bleeding and set her broken arm. We did have to give her some blood, but I think the outlook is good." He shook hands with Mr. Hamilton.

"My mom is down in the chapel. Could you go talk to her?" Elizabeth asked.

The doctor nodded, then turned and walked away.

"Thank You, God!" Elizabeth sang out.

"Amen," said Justin, grinning. He reached out and hugged Elizabeth.

She was glad when he kept his arm around her.

"This is such a relief!" Mr. Hamilton said, wiping his forehead with a handkerchief.

"Isn't it?" Elizabeth was so happy that Aunt Nan was going to be all right, she even felt a little warmth for Mr. Hamilton.

"I think I'll go drag your mom up here," Mr. Hamilton said. "I'll get some sodas or something too. Sound good?"

"I'll go with you and help carry," said Mike.

Elizabeth and Justin sat side by side on a sofa. Elizabeth realized she was still holding Dede's billfold. She turned it round and round, thinking. Her fingers slid closer and closer to the clasp until it seemed to just pop open.

"Oops!" she said but looked down to see what was inside. Dede's face stared up at her from a driver's license. Elizabeth looked a little closer. It was issued in New Mexico but to Susanna J. Cox—*SJC*. She quickly closed it.

"We still have time to get to the science fair ceremony," said Justin.

"You go ahead. I don't think I'll go. I want to see Aunt Nan."

"I'll stay too."

"No, you go on. Then you can call me and tell me if I won anything," said Elizabeth.

Justin stood slowly. "Are you sure? I'll stay if you want me to stay."

Elizabeth shook her head. "I won't be able to sleep tonight if I don't know who wins."

"Tell your Aunt Nan … tell her … I'll pray for her," Justin said in little more than a whisper.

Elizabeth felt the cold lump in her chest melt. "I will," she said.

As soon as she was sure Justin was out of sight, Elizabeth opened the billfold again. The license had a photo of Dede but the name was still *Susanna*. On the back, her blood type was listed as O positive. Where was Dede now?

Elizabeth quickly checked the charge cards. They weren't made out to Susanna or Dede. They all belonged to Nan Albright. How could Dede do this to Aunt Nan? How did she know all that stuff about Aunt Nan's family? And hardest of all, how were they going to tell Aunt Nan?

Mom came into the room, hanging onto Mr. Hamilton's arm. "Isn't it great?" she asked.

Elizabeth made herself smile.

"Dede still isn't back?" Mom asked, looking around. "And where's Justin?"

"He went to the science fair," said Elizabeth. "I don't know where Dede is."

"Oh, honey, the science fair. They're going to announce the winners soon, aren't they?" Mom looked at her watch. "You still have time to make it. Don will drive you there."

Elizabeth thought it over. She had no intention of going to the science fair, but she wanted to go back to the house and see if there was any sign of Dede. She probably should tell Mom about the billfold now, but why add that to everything Mom was already dealing with, especially after what she'd said earlier. Elizabeth had a feeling they might be rid of Dede for good after tonight.

"Aunt Nan would want you to go," Mom said.

"Okay." Elizabeth stood.

"I'll come right back," said Don.

"Mike, you ride along," Mom said. "And Lizzybeth, get a ride home with Meghan."

Elizabeth nodded.

In the car, Mike kept up a constant stream of chatter about sports. It was easy for Elizabeth to tune it out.

"Are you sure you don't want me to come in with you?" Mr. Hamilton asked.

"Mom needs to have someone with her now," said Elizabeth. She opened the car door and got out. "Thanks," she added.

Mr. Hamilton drove away. As soon as the car was out of sight, Elizabeth turned and started walking toward home as fast as she could.

12

THE CAMPER
WITH
EVERYTHING

The house was completely dark—Aunt Nan's side of the duplex and their side. Elizabeth had been so sure that she'd catch up with Dede at the house. Her steps slowed.

Elizabeth remembered she didn't have her key. She got the spare from under the flower pot and unlocked the door to her house. She dropped the billfold on the chair by the door, then slowly walked to the kitchen and filled a glass with water. Elizabeth drank it all, then filled it again. She let the water run cold, filled her hands and splashed it over her face.

How was she going to tell Aunt Nan that Dede was a fake? Elizabeth decided she'd tell Mom first and let Mom tell Aunt Nan.

The cats came into the kitchen meowing loudly.

"You haven't been fed, have you?" Elizabeth said. She leaned over and patted Tiger and Delores. They rubbed against her legs. Suddenly, they both crouched and their ears cocked forward. "What is it? Another kitty in your territory?" The two cats ran into the front room.

Elizabeth got a tin of cat food out of the cabinet and pulled the lid off. Then she heard it—a dog barking—and it sounded like the dog was right outside the front door.

The cats were circling in front of the door, their tails twice their normal size. Elizabeth pulled the door open, planning to chase the dog away.

"Hey, you," she said, but the rest of the words stuck in her throat. Dede was tying the large dog Elizabeth had seen her with Saturday to the porch railing.

Elizabeth tried to slam the door shut, but the cats had already moved in and she couldn't do it without hurting them.

"Hey, yourself," Dede said.

Elizabeth pressed the lock on the screen door and held onto the handle tightly while

Dede pulled from the other side. "Get out of the way," Elizabeth said to the cats, kicking at them. They were too excited by the dog to notice what she was doing. The dog was barking and pulling at his leash, trying to get at the cats.

A man with long black hair, wearing a suede cowboy-style hat trimmed with turquoise, came up the steps.

"Help me," Dede said, stepping away from the door.

The man gave a hard jerk and Elizabeth tumbled out the front door. The cats followed, staying just out of the dog's reach.

"Great, who's this?" the man asked, holding Elizabeth by the arm.

She tried to twist away, but he gripped her tighter.

"The kid I was telling you about. The one who kept sticking her nose in my business," said Dede. "What is it they say about curiosity? That it kills cats?" She looked at Tiger and Delores.

Elizabeth opened her mouth to scream. Someone would hear her ... right?

Dede lunged forward and put her hand over Elizabeth's mouth. "Don't do it. Not if you care about those irritating little balls of fur." She slowly removed her hand, but the man quickly put his in its place.

"Here, kitty, kitty." Dede knelt down and tried to coax the cats a little nearer.

Hot tears spilled over and ran down Elizabeth's cheeks.

"Ow!" Dede pulled away from the cats, sucking on the back of her hand. "It scratched me."

"Leave the cats alone," the man said. "What are we going to do with her?" He stuck his knee in Elizabeth's back.

"She's going to ruin everything. Bring her in the house while we search for that picture. I know it's here someplace."

The man pushed her in front of him into Aunt Nan's side of the duplex. He threw her down on the couch.

"We do have her to thank for something. If she hadn't mentioned the other night that I couldn't have type O blood and be related to Helen, I wouldn't have known to get out of the hospital when I did. Who would have thought that I would be called on to give blood? Thank you, Miss Bryan," Dede said sarcastically.

Elizabeth wished she'd never mentioned

blood types.

"The picture has to be down here. The only place I haven't looked is in Aunt Nan's room. She never gave me a chance. You watch her, and I'll go look right now. All that stuff beside the door is stuff we're taking with us," Dede said.

Elizabeth couldn't believe it. The duplex was completely torn apart. Pillows from the chairs were on the floor, books were off the shelves, even the rug was rolled up.

"What are you looking for? I might know where it is," Elizabeth said.

"Some painting," the man said. He was going through Aunt Nan's jewelry box, which was in the pile Dede had said they were taking with them.

"I found it!" There was no mistaking the victory in Dede's voice.

"That's what you've been looking for?" the man asked as Dede held it up proudly. It was a small framed picture of a stream running through some trees.

"It's worth a fortune," she said. "I can't believe how easy this whole thing has been— except for you." She turned and faced Elizabeth.

"Let's just get out of here," said the man.

"We have what we came for."

"And a little bit more. You know, she could ruin the whole thing," said Dede.

"Who are you?" Elizabeth asked.

"I'm Dede," she answered sweetly.

"Susanna J. Cox," said Elizabeth.

"How does she know that?" the man asked.

"Sasha," the woman corrected. "I'm Dede's little friend Sasha, and I spent as much time at her house as I did at my own. That means I know as much about Dede as Dede does. Except I also know that this picture is going to pay my way through art school. Poor Dede. It could have been her." Sasha laughed.

"Go on. I won't tell," Elizabeth said. "No one will be home for hours. You'll be far away by then."

"Like you don't know how to dial 911," said Sasha. "I've heard about your detective exploits."

"So let's give her some of that tea you gave to the old lady and get out of here. She won't wake up until we're two states away." The man was starting to sound impatient.

"I used it all," said Sasha. "We'll have to take her with us. We'll dump her out when we get far enough away. Now take a load of that stuff out to the camper."

Elizabeth was afraid. The last time she'd been in a tight situation at least Justin had been with her. This time she was all alone.

The dog was already sitting in the front seat of the truck—the same truck and camper she and Meghan had seen last week on the way home from school. When Sasha led Elizabeth out of the door, the cats were nowhere in sight. Elizabeth hoped they were all right.

"If you say anything, you'll be sorry. You saw how Rex pulled open your screen with one little jerk. Think what he could do to your hair," Sasha said right against Elizabeth's ear.

Elizabeth didn't *want* to think about it.

Sasha opened the door to the camper and pushed Elizabeth inside. Elizabeth stayed on the floor, listening to the engine roar to life. She rubbed her arm where Rex had held onto her, then pulled her knees up to her chest and rested her head on them.

Please God, help me. How do I get into these messes anyway? As she prayed, Elizabeth calmed slightly. She raised her head and looked around the inside of the camper. It was just as

Meghan had described—a refrigerator, a stove, a sofa. They turned a corner and Elizabeth lost her balance, falling over on her side. She heard pots and pans rattling around inside the cabinet. They made a big racket. She had an idea.

Elizabeth stood up and walked across to the kitchenette. It wasn't easy to keep her balance in a swaying vehicle, but she grabbed the counter with one hand and opened a cabinet with the other. Several pans tumbled out immediately. She caught them, then turned around.

In the very back of the trailer was a small window, not big enough to climb out of but big enough for the pans to fit through. Elizabeth pulled the curtains aside, opened the window, and waited for a car to pull up behind the camper.

The streets were dark and traffic was light. A few cars passed going the other way, but Elizabeth didn't think they'd notice the pots and pans if she simply threw them out onto the road. A car would have to come up behind the camper and have the utensils land on the hood.

They stopped, then started up again, passing through an intersection. Elizabeth knew they were approaching the edge of town. She saw tiny pinpoints of light approaching the trailer. At the same time, the camper picked up speed, and the lights soon disappeared.

Elizabeth saw a single light in the distance, then heard a buzz that sounded like a swarm of flies. The noise grew along with the size and intensity of the light, getting closer and closer. Elizabeth tensed, waiting for the motorcycle to get close enough.

It stayed just far enough back that she did-n't feel confident about throwing the pans. Again the trailer picked up speed, swaying from side to side. Elizabeth knew she had to be sure of getting the motorcyclist's attention the first time because if Sasha and Rex heard her, she would-n't get a second chance.

Elizabeth took a deep breath and stuck her arms, then her head as far out of the window as she could. "Hey, help me!" she yelled, letting go of the pots and pans right in the path of the motorcycle. The cycle swerved, then slowed. Elizabeth hung out the window, motioning for it to come closer.

A red light flashed, then a siren sounded.

Elizabeth pulled inside the camper quickly. She'd thrown pots and pans at a police officer!

13
BLUE RIBBONS

"This place is a mess!" Mom stood in the doorway, not taking a step inside Aunt Nan's house.

"Dede, I mean, Sasha did it looking for the oil painting," Elizabeth explained.

"We're going to have to clean it all up. And I don't want even a hint of it left for Aunt Nan to see," Mom said.

"I'll do it," Elizabeth volunteered.

Mom pulled the door shut, and they went into their own house.

"I don't know how much a person is expected to deal with in one day," Mom said, collapsing on the sofa.

"I'm sorry. I should have told you about the billfold, but you were so worried about Aunt Nan," Elizabeth said.

"To look up and see a police officer coming into the hospital chapel with you, your hair in tangles and your shirt ripped." Mom covered her face with her hands.

"I didn't know my shirt was ripped." Elizabeth tried to smooth her hair. She sat down beside her mother. "Honestly, I'm really, really sorry."

"But you stopped her." Mom sat up. "You stopped her from taking all of Aunt Nan's jewelry and her credit cards and her painting and …"

"I didn't ever like Dede," said Elizabeth. "When she was around you and Aunt Nan she was so nicey-nice, but she wasn't that way when she was with just me. And she threatened Tiger and Delores."

Mom laughed. "I can't believe I'm laughing about this. I must be totally exhausted," she said.

"Is Aunt Nan okay?" Elizabeth asked.

"She's fine."

"Did they find the blood she needed?"

"They did, even without Dede's."

Mom hugged Elizabeth. "Aunt Nan needed negative blood. That made it more difficult, plus they do like to have a perfect match if possible."

"I wonder what will happen to the dog?" Elizabeth asked.

"The dog?"

"Dede, Sasha, I mean, and Rex had a big

dog. They both had to go to jail so I wonder what will happen to the dog."

"I guess it will go to the pound."

"Oh, Mom!"

Mom sighed. "We can't have a dog."

"We can't let them do anything to it. It was a nice dog. But it didn't like the cats very much. Still, can't we at least call and make sure it's all right."

"Yes, yes. I'll call first thing in the morning. But now it's time for you to tell me about Dede."

"The very first day Dede was here, I heard her talking on the phone to somebody. Then when Aunt Nan asked her who it was, she lied.

"I also heard funny noises in the basement. It was Dede, or Sasha, and Rex moving stuff around, looking for the picture she wanted to steal. They were doing it while they had Aunt Nan drugged," said Elizabeth.

"Drugged!"

"That tea Dede kept feeding her."

"Nan thought there was something funny about the tea. That's why she tried to spend as much time with us as she could," said Mom.

"When I went to get the photo album, I saw Dede's suitcase. It had the initials *SJC* on it."

"Why didn't you say anything to any-body?" Mom interrupted.

"I didn't want to be accused of snooping. Besides, I knew everyone would come up with perfectly logical reasons to explain what was going on. I also saw Dede wearing Aunt Nan's earrings and kiss a guy in the park. Now I know it was Rex."

"You should have told us about that," said Mom.

"Anyway, when the nurse said Dede's blood type wasn't the same as Aunt Nan's and that it was type O, I got this picture in my mind of a Punnett square."

Mom looked puzzled.

"That's like the square in my science fair project," Elizabeth explained. "I remembered that Aunt Nan had said that her sister had type AB blood. I knew that Dede couldn't be an O.

"But the billfold clinched it. The driver's license was made out to *Susanna J. Cox*, but it had Dede's picture on it.

"Turns out she was Sasha, the little girl in the picture in Aunt Nan's album. That meant she knew a lot of what went on with Dede at the time her mother died. She ran into Dede recently, and they talked about the painting and how great it would be if Dede's mom had bought it instead of Aunt Nan. Then Dede could have had money to go to school. Sasha decided to find Aunt Nan and pretend to be Dede. She almost carried it off. She would have gotten away if I hadn't come home," Elizabeth said.

"Promise me you'll stop taking these chances. I'm turning into a nervous wreck wondering about you whenever you're out of my sight. If they'd thrown you out on the side of the road, no telling what would have happened to you."

"But they didn't," Elizabeth said.

Mom frowned.

"I promise not to do it again," Elizabeth said quickly.

"I'm beat. Let's try to get some sleep. Don will be here bright and early with Mike so he can get some clean clothes for school. It was so nice of him to take Mike home with him," said Mom.

The phone rang.

"What time is it?" Mom said, running to answer it. "Hello?"

"It's Justin, for you." Mom held the receiver out to Elizabeth.

"Hi," she answered. Elizabeth listened, a smile spreading across her face.

"Amy Catherine?" she asked, not hardly believing the answer.

"They're going to what?" Elizabeth had missed a lot at the science fair awards ceremony.

"Thanks for calling." She hung up the phone and turned to Mom with a big smile on her face.

"Blue ribbons," she said, dancing around the room. "For me, Justin, *and* Meghan. City-wide here we come!"

"Justin said a lot more than that," said Mom.

"Well, Amy Catherine withdrew her project. She told Mrs. Harms that she thought she'd gotten too much help from her parents, and she wanted to do another project on her own. That plus what happened to Rich ..."

"Rich?"

"A new guy. He did his project but wouldn't show it because he didn't have all the stuff everyone else had. He used a cardboard box for his poster and did it in crayon. I found the project in the trash and showed it to Mrs. Harms *after* she'd gotten all over him for not having a project.

"Anyway, we're going to do projects in class from now on," Elizabeth said.

"What a day!" said Mom.

"What a day," Elizabeth echoed.

"Can I sleep in your bed?" Elizabeth asked. Even though she knew Sasha and Rex were in jail, she didn't want to go upstairs alone.

"Sure," said Mom. "I could use a little company myself."

As soon as the two of them climbed in bed, Tiger and Delores jumped up and joined them.

"Elizabeth, we need to talk about Don too," Mom said.

Elizabeth closed her eyes and pretended to sleep.